# Turkey Claus

by

Wendi Silvano

illustrated by

Lee Harper

Amazon Children's Publishing

To the love of my life . . . Eddy

—W.S.

To my dog, Dash, who thinks all my
drawings are great

—L.H.

Text copyright © 2012 by Wendi Silvano
Illustrations copyright © 2012 by Lee Harper

All rights reserved
Amazon Publishing
Attn: Amazon Children's Books
P.O. Box 400818
Las Vegas, NV 89149
www.amazon.com/amazonchildrenspublishing

Library of Congress Cataloging-in-Publication Data

Silvano, Wendi J.
Turkey Claus / by Wendi Silvano ; illustrated by Lee Harper. — 1st ed.
p. cm.
Summary: Santa Claus finds a way to help Turkey avoid becoming Christmas
dinner.
ISBN 978-0-7614-6239-2 (hardcover) — ISBN 978-0-7614-6240-8 (ebook)
[1. Turkeys—Fiction. 2. Santa Claus—Fiction. 3. Christmas—Fiction. 4.
Costume—Fiction.]  I. Harper, Lee, 1960- ill. II. Title.
PZ7.S585645Tr 2012
[E]—dc23
2011034874

The illustrations are rendered in watercolor and pencil on 140 lb. Arches
hot press watercolor paper.
Book design by Anahid Hamparian
Editor: Robin Benjamin

Printed in China (W)
First edition
1 3 5 6 4 2

**Thanksgiving was over, and Turkey was safe.**
But then he overheard Farmer Jake and his wife, Edna, talking about what to have for Christmas dinner. And guess who was at the top of the list?

"I do love a nice turkey dinner," said Edna.

*Oh, no,* thought Turkey. *Not again!*
But Turkey had an idea. . . .

The children had mailed their Christmas wishes to Santa Claus. Maybe Turkey could ask Santa for a Christmas wish, too. . . . A wish that he would *not* be eaten for Christmas dinner!

But it was too late to mail his wish to Santa. Turkey would have to go see Santa himself.

Turkey arrived at Santa's Village. "Excuse me," said Turkey. "Where can I find Santa?"

"No one sees Santa the day before Christmas," said an elf. "He's too busy making his list and checking it twice."

"Oh, gobble, gobble," said Turkey.

But looking around gave Turkey a new idea. What if he didn't look like a turkey? What if he looked like a Christmas tree? Surely a Christmas tree could get to see Santa.

STARS

LIGHTS

His costume wasn't bad. In fact, Turkey
looked just like a Christmas tree . . . almost.

"Ho . . . Ho . . . HOLD IT!" cried the elf. "No turkeys in Santa's Village. You have to go back to the farm!"

"How'd you know it was me?" asked Turkey.

"Trees don't have legs," said the elf.

"Oh, gobble, gobble," groaned Turkey.

Turkey looked around again. *I've got it!* he thought. Surely a reindeer could get to see Santa.

His costume wasn't bad. In fact, Turkey looked just like a reindeer . . .

. . . almost.

"Halt your hooves!" cried an elf. "No turkeys allowed in Santa's Village today. You have to go back to the farm!"

"Oh, how could you tell it was me?" asked Turkey.

"Reindeer don't have wings," said the elf.

"Oh, gobble, gobble," moaned Turkey. "I've got to see Santa!"

Turkey looked around for another idea. Candy was
being loaded into Santa's sleigh. *I've got it!* he thought.
Surely a candy cane would be allowed inside with Santa.

His costume wasn't bad. In fact, Turkey looked just like a candy cane . . . almost.

"Wait a merry minute!" cried an elf. "Turkeys are *not* candy. You have to go back to the farm!"

"How could you tell it was me?" asked Turkey.

"Candy canes don't have beaks," said the elf.

"Oh, gobble, gobble," howled Turkey. "I just *have* to get in to see Santa!"

Turkey looked around and around. He saw Mrs. Claus bring a plate of cookies to the elves.

Surely . . . surely Mrs. Claus could get in to see Santa.

His costume wasn't bad. In fact, Turkey looked just like Mrs. Claus . . . almost.

Turkey walked right up to Santa's house. An elf opened the door.

"Snow way!" said the elf. "No turkey is getting in here today!"

"How'd you recognize me?" wailed Turkey.

"Mrs. Claus doesn't have feathers," said the elf.

"Oh, gobble, gobble, gobble." Turkey sighed. "I'm almost out of time. I'll never get to ask Santa for my wish."

Turkey looked around desperately for one last idea.
Then he saw it.

His costume wasn't bad. In fact, it was his best yet. . . .

**Ding-dong.** An elf brought in the box.

"What's this?" said Santa. "A present for me?"

Out popped Turkey. "Merry Christmas!" he cried. "Gobble, gobble!"

"HO . . . HO . . . HO! HA . . . HA . . . HA!" laughed Santa. "What are you doing here, Turkey?"

Turkey explained his Christmas wish.
Santa smiled. "I think I have just the right disguise for you."

And he did.

It was Turkey's best Christmas ever!